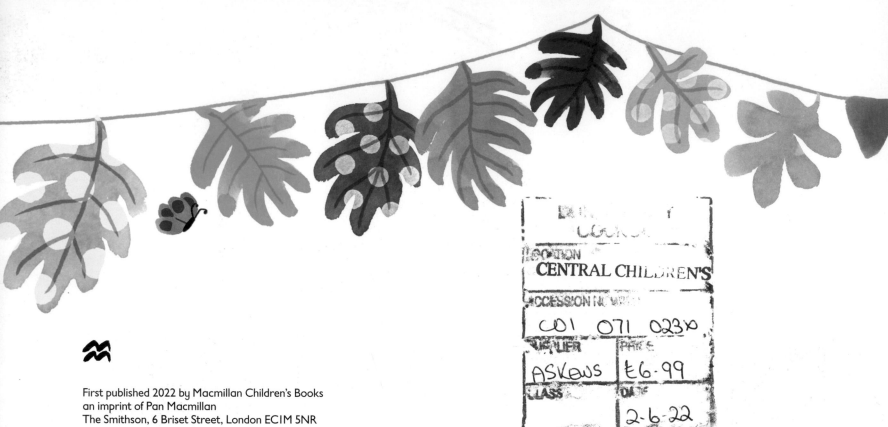

First published 2022 by Macmillan Children's Books
an imprint of Pan Macmillan
The Smithson, 6 Briset Street, London EC1M 5NR
EU representative: Macmillan Publishers Ireland Limited
1st Floor, The Liffey Trust Centre, 117–126 Sheriff Street Upper, Dublin 1, D01 YC43
Associated companies throughout the world

www.panmacmillan.com

ISBN: 978-1-5290-8475-7

Text copyright © Macmillan Children's Books 2022
Illustrations copyright © Alberta Torres 2022

The right of Alberta Torres to be identified as the illustrator
of this work has been asserted by her in accordance with
the Copyright, Designs and Patents Act 1988.

9 8 7 6 5 4 3 2 1

A CIP catalogue record for this book is available
from the British Library.

Printed in China

This Little DINOSAUR

Coral Byers

Alberta Torres

Macmillan Children's Books

This little dinosaur **stamps** and **stomps**

abc

1

This little dinosaur
swoops and **soars**

2

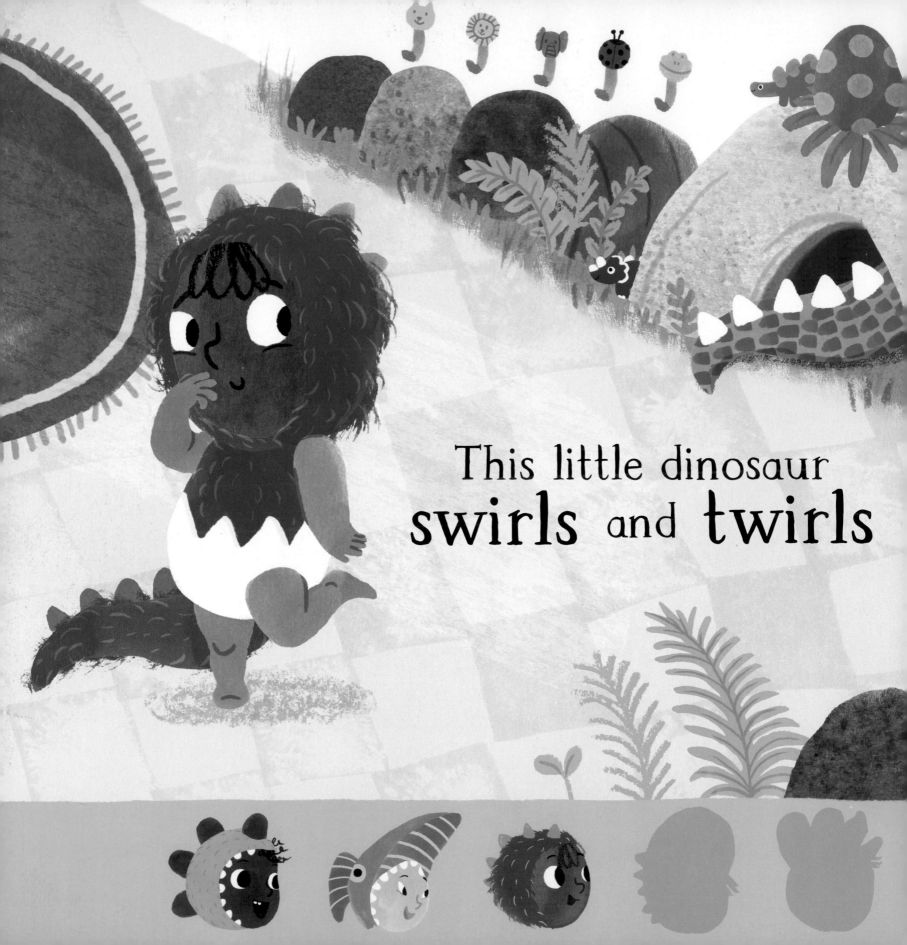

This little dinosaur
swirls and twirls

3

And this little dinosaur
ROARS!

4

This little dinosaur
wants to hide

This little dinosaur
plays along

6

This little dinosaur
counts to ten ...

Where have all the
dinosaurs gone?

7

This little dinosaur's
busy building

This little dinosaur
wants to play!

This little dinosaur
hears a noise...

KABOOM!

They all run away!

10

And all the little dinosaurs go...

ROAR ROAR

All the way home!

Reading Together
Tips for Parents and Carers

This book has been specially created and developed for preschool children.
It uses the popular nursery rhyme *This Little Piggy* to create an
instantly familiar, read-aloud preschool adventure!

- The fun, repetitive and rhythmic text helps develop language
  and vocabulary.

- The bar along the bottom counts from 1 to 10, with
  numbers on each page to help children recognize numerals.

- The children in this book are in a nursery classroom.
  This can help children get used to – and excited about –
  starting formal childcare or preschool themselves.

- There is plenty of evidence to show that sharing books and
  reading together helps children to communicate, develop
  ideas and understanding, and gives them a head start at
  school. But the most important thing is to enjoy the
  closeness of sharing a book together.

When you read this book together, you could talk to your child about...

...the ten children in the book. Can your child find and count each one as you go along? **What is each child doing?** You could encourage your child to join in and mimic the children's actions.

...how the children's world changes into **an imaginative make-believe world** as they play. What can your child see change as they turn the pages?

...things around you that your child could use to **create their own make-believe world.** What would they like to dress up as?

...the numbers in the book – can they find and **read each number?** Try reading the book while your child counts each little dinosaur on their fingers or toes, just like in the nursery rhyme.

Say Hello to the Dinosaurs!

1  **Max** always wants to be first!

2  **Iris** loves to dance.

3  **Aisha** can count all the way to 100!

4  **Muhammed** can shout really loudly!

5  **Grace** loves to play hide-and-seek.

6  **Benjamin** is really good at jumping high.

7  **Noa**'s favourite colour is blue.

8  **Evie** likes to play football and go swimming.

9  **Ezra**'s favourite food is cake.

10  **Felix** loves to build tall towers.

What will they all dress up as next?